We Lost a Sock

We Lost a Sock

Written by
Claire Falloon

Illustrated by
Rohan Daniel Eason

Cool Hippies Books

We Lost a Sock

Published by Cool Hippies Books

Copyright © 2023 by Claire Falloon

All rights reserved. Neither this book, nor any parts within it may be sold or reproduced in any form or by any electronic or mechanical means, including information storage and retrieval systems, without permission in writing from the author. The only exception is by a reviewer, who may quote short excerpts in a review.

Library of Congress Control Number: 2023948882

ISBN (hardcover): 9781662942242

ISBN (paperback): 9781662942259

eISBN: 9781662942266

For my family: Bruce, Miles, Ice Cube, and Yoko - CLF

For my son, Fox Wilhelm Lewis - RDE

We lost a sock along the way.
Where it went to, I can't say.
We'll try and find it anyway.
Will you help us look today?

Now, let's think, where might it hide?
Is our sock up on that slide?
Or on the whirly-roundy ride?
No, that sock we have not spied . . .

We lost a sock along the way.
Where it went to, I can't say.
We'll try and find it anyway.
Will you help us look today?

Is it out? Is it in?
Is it floating on the wind?

Our patience now is wearing thin . . .
Where, oh where, is this sock's twin?

Is it low? Is it high?
Did they bake it in a pie?
Is it on some other guy?
We can find it if we try!

We lost a sock along the way.
Where it went to, I can't say.
We'll try and find it anyway.
Will you help us look today?

Wait a minute—stop the clock!
Did our pup just find the sock?
Now if his jaws will just unlock . . .
finally, our search can stop!

Printed in the USA
CPSIA information can be obtained
at www.ICGtesting.com
LVHW061738230124
769627LV00011B/331